Sight Word Tales ™

Come to the Zany Zoo

MVFOL

by Jane Quinn
illustrated by Jim Paillot

SCHOLASTIC INC.

New York • Toronto • London • Auckland • Sydney
Mexico City • New Delhi • Hong Kong • Buenos Aires

Designed by Maria Lilja
ISBN-13: 978-0-545-01645-2 • ISBN-10: 0-545-01645-2
Copyright © 2007 by Scholastic Inc.
All rights reserved. Printed in the U.S.A.

First printing, October 2007

12 11 10 9 8 7 6 5 4 3 2   40   9 10 11 12/0

Welcome to the **ZaNY ZOO**
COME ON IN!

Sight Words

Sight words are words that you see again and again when you read. This book is filled with the sight words **come**, **to**, **the**, and **see**. Look for them in the text. Check the pictures, too!

Come to the zany zoo!
Come see the polka-dot kangaroo!

Come to the zany zoo!
Come see the hippo in a tutu!

Come to the zany zoo!
Come see the flamingo in one pink shoe!

Come to the zany zoo!
Come see the elephant in a canoe!

Come to the zany zoo!
Come see the panda play peek-a-boo!

Come to the zany zoo!
Come see the leopard play a kazoo!

Come to the zany zoo!
Come see the bear make things with glue!

Come to the zany zoo!
Come see the alligator add two plus two!

Come to the zany zoo!
Come see the tiger who only says, "Moo!"

Come to the zany zoo!
Come see the zebra who is red, white, and blue!

Come to the zany zoo!
Come see the lion with a fancy hairdo!

Come to the zany zoo!
Come see the animals.
They want **to see** you!

Sight Word Review

Do you know the four sight words in this book? Read aloud the word on each shoe.

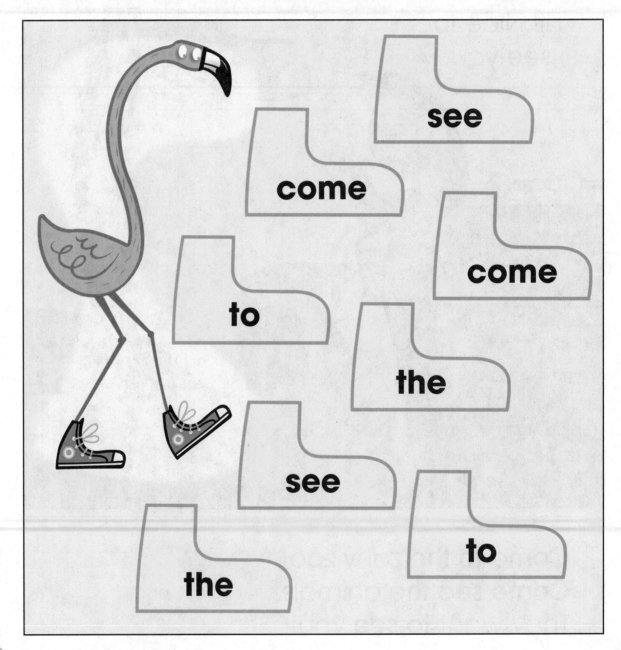

Sight Word Fill-ins

Listen to the sentences. Then choose a sight word from the box to fill in each blank.

Word Box	**come**	**to**	**the**	**see**

1. Can I _____ with you?

2. He will _____ his aunt next week.

3. The teacher told us not _____ run.

4. She cannot _____ over today.

5. I will be a fairy in _____ play.

6. Did you _____ that big bug?

7. We love _____ have picnics.

8. Let's go on _____ swings.

Answers: 1. come 2. see 3. to 4. come 5. the 6. see 7. to 8. the

Sight Word Cheers

Celebrate the new sight words you learned by saying these four short cheers.

C-o-m-e! Give a yell!
What do these four letters spell?
A sight word that we all know well —
Come, come, come!

T-o! Give a yell!
What do these two letters spell?
A sight word that we all know well —
To, to, to!

T-h-e! Give a yell!
What do these three letters spell?
A sight word that we all know well —
The, the, the!

S-e-e! Give a yell!
What do these three letters spell?
A sight word that we all know well —
See, see, see!